The Rosary:
The John Paul II
Method

2nd Edition
(Revised)

The Rosary:
The John Paul II Method

2nd Edition
(Revised)

By
Robert Feeney

AQUINAS
PRESS

Nihil Obstat: Reverend Paul F. deLadurantaye, S.T.D.
                Censor Librorum

Imprimatur: ✠ Most Reverend Michael F. Burbidge
                Bishop of Arlington
                March 1, 2017

The nihil obstat and imprimatur are official declarations that a book or pamphlet is free from doctrinal or moral error. No implication is contained therein that those who grant the nihil obstat or imprimatur agree with the contents or statements expressed.

Scripture quotations are from the Revised Standard Version Bible Catholic Edition, Copyright 1965 and 1966 by the Division of Christian Education of the National Council of the Churches of Christ in the U.S.A.

Cover Photo- Photo Services, L'Osservatore Romano
Photo credits: Photos of the 20 mysteries are taken, with permission, from the booklet *Praying the Rosary without distractions* by the Rosary Center, Portland, Oregon.

To Mary, the *Lady of the Rosary*, for
the glory of the Lord, for the good of
souls and of His Church.

To my lovely and dearest daughter,
Mary Ann

To all of my students I've taught over the years

To the young, who through praying the Rosary will
become the light of the world and the salt of the earth,
and will radiate the beauty of Christ

Acknowledgments

Special appreciation goes to Cardinal Edwin F. O'Brien for his Foreword. Thanks also go to Archbishop Joseph E. Kurtz for his Prefatory Note. Special thanks go to the Carthusian monks of Arlington, VT, and the many contemplative nuns who pray for the spiritual success of this book. Thanks go to Kimberley Anderson for her typesetting of the manuscript. Thanks also to Jim Welsford and Anne Keran for their editorial assistance.

Author's Note

In this 2017 printing of the revised 2nd edition, celebrating the 100th anniversary of the Marian apparitions at Fatima, there is mention of John Paul II's canonization by Pope Francis. Wherever "Blessed" John Paul II was mentioned previously, it has now been changed to "Saint" John Paul II. Some additional changes have also been made.

Contents

Prefatory Note by Archbishop Joseph E. Kurtz................8

Foreword by Cardinal Edwin F. O'Brien...........…..…..........9

1. The Origin of the Rosary.....................................…......11

2. The School of Mary...…....15

3. Fatima and the Rosary...............................……......21

4. The Rosary and Contemplation.............…..........…......26

5. The John Paul II Method...................…...................…...28

6. The 20 Mysteries ....…..........32

Appendix ....…..........72

Notes ....…...........80

Prefatory Note

"Mr. Feeney has done a great service in bringing to life for the modern individual the spiritual legacy of the Holy Rosary. By capturing the vision of Pope Saint John Paul II that the Holy Rosary leads us "… to contemplate with Mary the face of Christ," this book opens the door for a spiritual life enriched by this time-honored devotion. By detailing the way in which our late Holy Father approached the daily prayer of the Rosary, he gives us a concrete example to follow. All who read it will be indebted for this fine work."

Most Reverend Joseph E. Kurtz, D.D.
Archbishop of Louisville

Foreword

In this age when the discipline of prayer seems lost for so many, the recitation of the Rosary offers an excellent framework within which to renew that discipline. This work on Saint John Paul II's method of praying the Rosary is a great primer for what the late Pope called "the school of Mary." Students of this "school" will find their relationship with Jesus and Mary deeply enriched.

Robert Feeney exposes the rich history of the Rosary, highlighting the encouragement the Blessed Mother gave at Fatima to "pray the Rosary every day," as well as the teaching that St. John Paul II gave to us on the devotion.

Not only is the Rosary a powerful prayer for peace in our world and the end to war, it can also bring an interior peace in one's spiritual life. Those who undertake the contemplation of the face of Christ in Mary's company using the method explained here are certain to be nourished by rich spiritual food.

Edwin Cardinal O'Brien
Archbishop Emeritus of Baltimore

Our Lady of the Rosary

Chapter 1
The Origin of the Rosary

The Catholic Church, through her popes, attributes the institution of the Rosary to St. Dominic. In 1875, Blessed Pope Pius IX taught that Mary entrusted the Rosary to St. Dominic to use as a "weapon" in battling the monstrous errors *infecting* the world. In 1891, Leo XIII, the "Pope of the Rosary," who wrote 11 Rosary encyclicals, taught that it was at Mary's prompting and suggesting that St. Dominic introduced, preached, and used the Rosary to accomplish so much *good* in the world.

The origin of the Rosary is rooted in the thirteenth century. At that time, France was threatened by the Albigensian heresy, which believed that matter was evil and the spirit was good. The Albigensians believed that all life on earth—being the work of Satan—was evil. Their anti-life attitude produced a culture of death. In 1208, after much fruitless labor preaching to the Albigensians in southern France, the revelation of the Rosary to St. Dominic took place.

At the time of the revelation of the Rosary to him, St. Dominic was a 36-year-old priest from Calaruega, Spain. He was a man of great character, well-educated and lovable, being light of heart and playful. He was always radiant and joyous, except when moved to compassion by some misfortune of his neighbors. As he grew older he became more boyish. He loved the young and they, in turn, were attracted to him and his outlook on life. He believed in the young and their potential to do great things for God and to climb instantly to places of importance. He is described as being of middle height, and his presence was attractive with a very handsome face, blond hair, and a ruddy complexion. A brilliant radiance came from his head, which attracted many to love and respect him. He was known for his tremendous physical endurance and was described as "the strong athlete." His athletic body retained its youthfulness and flexibility under the physical efforts of his many days of *endless* walking.

At the time of the Rosary revelation to him in 1208, St. Dominic was praying in the chapel of St. Mary in *Prouille*, southern France. He was tearfully complaining to Mary about the poor fruit of his preaching to the Albigensians. In the midst of his lament, Mary appeared to him and said:

"Wonder not that until now you have obtained so little fruit by your labors: You have spent them on a barren soil, not yet watered with the dew of divine grace. When God willed to renew the face of the earth, He began by sending down on it the fertilizing rain of the Angelic Salutation. Preach my Psalter (Rosary) composed of 150 Angelic Salutations and 15 Our Fathers and you will obtain an abundant harvest."[1]

Mary taught Dominic this method of praying and ordered him to preach it far and wide. It is said of Dominic that he would go from town to town in France, Spain, and Italy and preach the Rosary. He established the *Confraternity of the Rosary* (see appendix) in nearly every town he preached. Dominic would meditate on the mysteries of the life, death, and resurrection of Jesus found in the Gospel, following the example of Mary, who pondered the mysteries of her Son in her heart. His meditations would be interspersed with praying 15 Our Fathers and 150 Hail Marys. He would preach to the people on these mysteries. After the people reflected on each mystery, Dominic would then invite his hearers to take up the string of knots or beads and to pray a decade of the Our Father and ten Hail Marys. Blessed Pope Pius IX, who declared the Immaculate Conception a dogma of faith in 1854, taught that St. Dominic used the Rosary as a *sword* to destroy the errors of the Albigensian heresy. He taught that if the faithful used the Rosary like St. Dominic did, then the many errors and evils infecting the world would be uprooted and destroyed.

Dominic, the "holy athlete" and a "true light of the world," died on August 6, 1221, at the age of 51, in Bologna, Italy, where he is buried in a basilica bearing his name. Dominic had set the world aflame, and the memory of his name has never been forgotten. He was like a "David" of old, using the Rosary as a "slingshot," a weapon against evil. He was like a doctor, using the Rosary as a "serum," injecting all the afflicted with it so that vices would be rooted out and virtues infused. His followers, the *Dominicans*, have followed the example of St. Dominic throughout the centuries in bringing the *Rosary of Mary* to the people.

Both Pope Leo XIII and Pius XI accepted the chapel of St. Mary at Prouille in southern France as the place where St. Dominic received the revelation of the Rosary. Today in Prouille, the "cradle of the Rosary" as Pope Pius XI called it, there is an international monastery of Dominican contemplative nuns, a retreat house, and a grand basilica in honor of *Our Lady of the Rosary*. It is in a beautiful setting at the foot of the quaint town of Fanjeaux, not far from Toulouse.

The fixing of definite mysteries was a long process that took centuries to develop and determine. St. Pope Pius V, a Dominican who in 1569 set into place the joyful, sorrowful, and glorious mysteries, finalized this process. On October 16, 2002, St. Pope John Paul II made an addition to the traditional 15 mysteries. He added five new mysteries called the *Mysteries of Light*. They include the mysteries of Jesus's public ministry between his Baptism and his Passion. He believed that when meditating upon the "Mysteries of Light" we turn the *beam* of Christ's light on the conflicts, tensions, and dramas of the five continents. He wrote that the addition of these new mysteries is meant to give the Rosary fresh life and to enkindle renewed interest in the Rosary as a true doorway to the depths of the Heart of Christ.

St. John Paul II wrote in his Rosary letter, "At times when Christianity itself seemed under threat, its deliverance was attributed to the power of this prayer, and Our Lady of the Rosary was acclaimed as the one whose intercession brought salvation" (no. 39). A good example of this would be the battle of Lepanto. In the 1560s, Turkish forces threatened Europe and the Sultan Selim sought to take the cross down from atop St. Peter's in Rome and replace it with a Muslim crescent. St. Pope Pius V launched a crusade of prayer. He asked all Catholics to pray the Rosary for success in stopping the advances of the Muslims.

During the worst part of the battle of Lepanto, fought on October 7, 1571, off the coast of Nafpoktos, Greece, the Christians were greatly outnumbered and faced destruction. A strong wind came up at that moment and caused the Turkish fleet to be in complete disarray. This led to their defeat. The Christian sailors had regularly been praying the Rosary along with Catholics throughout Europe.

On the same day, October 7, 1571, St. Pius V stood up at four o'clock in the afternoon during a conclave of cardinals. His face glowed with a strange light and he announced, "This is no time for business. Go and thank God. Our fleet has just won the victory."[2] St. Pope Pius V attributed the victory to praying the Rosary. The Venetian Senate wrote, "It was not generals nor battalions nor arms that brought us victory, but it was *Our Lady of the Rosary*."

In his letter on the Rosary, St. John Paul II mentioned the *Dominicans* using the Rosary at difficult times for the Church due to the spread of heresy. He mentioned two Dominicans, in particular, both of whom were members of the Dominican Third Order, consisting of laypeople, diocesan priests, and bishops. One of these great Third Order Dominicans was St. Louis de Montfort, who lived in France in the 15th century. St. John Paul II mentioned him as the author of an excellent book on the Rosary called *The Secret of the Rosary*. The other Third Order member was Blessed Bartolo Longo, a layman who was a lawyer living in 20th century Italy. The Pope mentioned that Longo promoted the Christocentric and contemplative heart of the Rosary. On October 19, 2008, at the world-famous Rosary Shrine in Pompeii, Italy, Benedict XVI called attention to Blessed Bartolo's *charism* of being an "apostle of the Rosary." The Pope taught us that Bartolo accepted the Rosary as a "true gift" from Mary's Heart, and that it was the *source* of his energy and perseverance.

Another great Third Order Dominican living in 20th century Italy, though not mentioned in the Rosary letter, was the young Blessed Pier Georgio Frassati. In 1990, St. John Paul II beatified this handsome and strong athlete who, in God's eyes, could easily be considered the greatest well-rounded athlete who ever lived. St. John Paul II called him the "model of athletes" in 1984. Bl. Pier Georgio loved praying the Rosary and encouraged others to pray it. He joined the *Confraternity of the Rosary* at age 17, a confraternity established by St. Dominic in the 13th century (more on the confraternity in appendix). Pier Georgio died right before graduating from his university studies in Turin at age 24. He died with a Rosary in his hand and a smile on his face.

Benedict XVI taught us that the image of Our Lady of the Rosary, as seen at the beginning of this chapter, shows that the Rosary is a means given by Mary to *contemplate* Jesus, to *meditate* on his life, to *love* him, and to *follow* him ever more faithfully.

Chapter 2

The School of Mary

On October 16, 2002, St. John Paul II signed his inspiring Apostolic Letter, *The Rosary of the Virgin Mary*. Three years later, Benedict XVI *highly* recommended that we reread John Paul II's letter on the Rosary (see excerpts in appendix) and put his directions into practice. Benedict XVI beatified John Paul II on May 1, 2011, declaring him "Blessed." Pope Francis canonized him a saint on April 27, 2014. Benedict XVI called him the great "Apostle of the Rosary." He saw a providential revival, a "new springtime" of the Rosary, thanks to John Paul II's example and his teaching on the Rosary. In 1985, Pope Francis (then Fr. Jorge Bergoglio, S.J.) attended a Rosary that was led by John Paul II. Seeing him on his knees, his Rosary in his hands, immersed in the contemplation of Christ, made such a deep impression on him that he decided that from that day on he would pray fifteen mysteries (three Rosaries) every day. Francis says, "the Rosary is the prayer that always accompanies my life. . . it is the prayer of my heart."

From his youth, the Rosary held an important place in St. John Paul II's spiritual life. It accompanied him during moments of difficulty and those of joy. He entrusted any number of concerns to the Rosary and always found comfort in it. St. John Paul II admitted, "The Rosary is my *favorite* prayer. A marvelous prayer! Marvelous in its simplicity and its *depth*. It can be said that the Rosary is, in some sense, a prayer-commentary on the final chapter of the Vatican II Constitution *Lumen Gentium*, a chapter which discusses the wondrous presence of the Mother of God in the mystery of Christ and the Church" (no. 2). In his letter on the Rosary, he wrote that "through the Rosary the faithful receive abundant grace, as though from the very hands of the Mother of the Redeemer" (no. 1). He noted that throughout his papacy he received *many* graces from Mary through praying the Rosary.

In his 2002 letter on the Rosary, St. John Paul II introduced us to a new method of praying the Rosary to help us pray it authentically—in a truly *meditative* way. This new method will lead to a friendship, an encounter with Jesus, in the 20 mysteries of the Rosary (Ch. 6). When this happens, we allow Mary, in her

15

ministry as mother, to train and mold our hearts until our great *friend,* Jesus, is fully formed in us. In May of 2008, Benedict XVI stated, "The Rosary is experiencing a 'new springtime.' It needs to be prayed in an authentic way, not mechanical and superficial, but profoundly."[4] In this "new springtime" of the Rosary, the *John Paul II Method* will assist us in praying this meditative prayer authentically, as Benedict XVI exhorted us to do. May all Dominicans, bishops, priests, deacons, and teachers promote this new method (Ch. 5) so that all can learn it, especially parents, who can then *teach* it to their children, the future and hope of the Church and humanity.

The late Holy Father encouraged *all* of us to pray the Rosary properly; otherwise, he wrote that there is a risk that the Rosary will fail to produce the intended spiritual effects. People who come to pray the Rosary according to St. John Paul's new method will less likely fall into such a risk.

In his letter, St. John Paul II states: "With the Rosary, the Christian people sit at the school of Mary and are led to contemplate the beauty on the face of Christ and to experience the depths of his love" (no. 1). He asks the question, "Could we have any better teacher than Mary? No one knows Christ any better than Mary; no one can introduce us to a profound knowledge of his mystery better than his mother" (no. 14). The Rosary is a marvelous school wherein Mary introduces us to Christ as she did to the shepherds and wise men. In her school, Mary reveals the beauty on the face of Christ to us through the 20 mysteries of the Rosary which appear in Ch. 6. This splendid school will ensure, as *Vatican II* stated: "When the Mother is honored, the Son…is rightly known, loved, and glorified" (Lumen Gentium, 66).

Many popes have praised Mary's Rosary as a "spiritual training school." Like a good coach's training program, St. John Paul II's new method of praying the Rosary (Chapters 5 and 6) can surely be the "training program" that can be implemented in order to help train and to win back strong "muscles" of the spirit that have often gone flabby and atrophied. Not only will students in Mary's "spiritual training school" use the Rosary to win back strong spiritual muscles, muscles needed today to be victorious in the great "battle of life," but they can also use it to be able to put into practice what the great St. Catherine of Siena, an Italian Third Order Dominican, once said: "If you are what you are meant to be, you will set the whole world on fire."[5]

The Rosary is also a most effective school of evangelization. St. John Paul II noted in his letter that the Rosary offers a spiritual and educational opportunity for the "new evangelization." He noted that the Rosary can present a significant catechetical opportunity when it combines all the elements needed for an effective meditation (Ch.6). He masterfully described the Rosary as "offering the 'secret' which leads easily to a profound and inward knowledge of Christ. We might call it *Mary's way*" (no. 26). He wrote that "the Rosary is a valuable resource for every good evangelizer" (no. 17). Oh, how the Rosary could be a most effective and far-reaching instrument for evangelization in the 21st century! St. John Paul II states, "Today we are facing new challenges. Why should we not once more have recourse to the Rosary?" (no. 17). The Rosary could surely offer the "secret" for *rekindling* the "light of faith" in the world and for re-evangelizing the West, which has been so negatively influenced by "secular humanism."

In his message for World Youth Day 2000 in Rome, St. John Paul II wrote, "Young people of every continent, do not be afraid to be the saints of the new millennium. Be contemplative and love prayer."[6] He taught that the contemplation of the mystery of Jesus, as we do in the mysteries of the Rosary (Ch.6), is genuine "training in holiness." The Rosary is truly a contemplative prayer. If the *art* of praying it prayerfully and meditatively (Ch.6) is put into practice, then it could surely shape the lives of the potential saints of the 3rd millennium. St. John Paul II encouraged the young to esteem the Rosary and to *delight* in praying it. At World Youth Day 2003, the "Year of the Rosary," he told the young that he was, in spirit, handing them the Rosary beads. He said, "To recite the Rosary means to learn to gaze on Jesus with his Mother's eyes and to love Jesus with his Mother's heart. Through prayer and meditation on the mysteries, Mary leads you safely towards her Son."[7] He also told the young, "Do not be ashamed to recite the Rosary alone, while you walk along the streets to school, to the university or to work, or as you commute by public transport. Adopt the habit of reciting it among yourselves, in your groups, movements, and associations. Do not hesitate to suggest that it be recited by your parents and brothers and sisters, because it rekindles and strengthens the bonds between them. This prayer will help you to be strong in your faith, constant in charity, joyful and persevering in hope."[8]

Pope Pius XII compared the Rosary to the "slingshot" of the young David, with which he overcame Goliath. It is interesting to note that in September 2007, Benedict XVI said, "The world must be changed, but it is precisely the *mission* of young people to change it." Today, the young can use the Rosary, like the young David used the slingshot, to "battle" against modern "Goliaths" such as immorality, the "culture of death," materialism, secularism, and the "dictatorship of relativism," and thus change the world as Benedict XVI exhorted them to do. St. John Paul II, Benedict XVI, and Pope Francis describe the Rosary as an effective "spiritual weapon" to be used in the "battle" against evil and violence. On October 6, 2010, Benedict XVI invited the young to make the Rosary their daily prayer. In accepting this invitation, the young, who are the hope and future of the Church and humanity, will obtain the graces, courage, and light needed to vigorously proclaim their faith in God and to "swim against the tide" by standing up for and defending the *true*, the *good*, and the *beautiful*.

The Rosary can help us to respond to Vatican II's "call to holiness." We can grow in holiness through a friendship, an encounter with our great *friend,* Jesus, in the 20 mysteries. St. John Paul II was convinced that the Rosary, prayed with meditation on the mysteries (Ch.6), can be a genuine path and a simple way to grow in holiness, which is the vocation of every baptized person. In his letter on the Rosary, he noted that "training in holiness" calls for "a Christian life distinguished above all in the art of prayer" (no. 5). He emphasized that the meditation on the mystery of Jesus is the most important reason for strongly encouraging the praying of the Rosary.

In his encouraging letter, St. John Paul II wrote about the urgent need today to counter a certain crisis concerning the Rosary which can cause it to be devalued and, therefore, no longer taught to the younger generation. He believed that if the Rosary is well-presented, the young would surprise adults and make it their own and pray it with *enthusiasm*. He wrote that perhaps the reason that the young are not attracted to the Rosary is the *impoverished* way it is presented and prayed. As we all know, the young look for *authenticity*, the "real deal." He also taught that there is nothing to stop the young from praying the Rosary if *practical aids* are offered to help them. St. John Paul II's practical suggestions (Ch.5) in the way the Rosary is prayed will *definitely* help the young and will overall improve the way the Rosary is prayed today. He wrote that the Rosary, as a method of contemplation, can be *improved*. In this new method, we can all find what the young call the "real deal."

St. John Paul II also wrote in his letter that he hoped that the Rosary would again be a prayer *of and for the family*. He mentioned that the family is being menaced by *forces of disintegration* today so as to make us fear for the future of not only the family, but of society as a whole. He wrote that the revival of the Rosary in Christian families would be an effective aid to countering the devastating effects of this crisis. He noted in his letter that at one time the Rosary was very dear to Christian families and it certainly brought them closer together. He stressed the need today for us to return to the praying of the Rosary and not to lose this precious *inheritance*. He wrote that "the family that prays the Rosary *together* place Jesus at the center; they place their needs and their plans in his hands; they draw from him the *hope* and *strength* to go on" (no. 41). St. John Paul II encouraged parents to entrust to the Rosary the growth and development of their children and to pray the Rosary for them and, even more, *with them*. He urged parents to train their children from the earliest years to experience this daily "pause for prayer" with the family.

St. John Paul II described the Rosary as a prayer loved by *countless* saints who discovered in the Rosary a genuine path to growth in holiness. He mentioned two of these saints by name in his letter. One was St. Padre Pio, who faithfully prayed many Rosaries every day and said on the day before he died, "Love Our Lady and help others to love her. Always recite the Rosary."[10] When asked what inheritance he wished to leave his spiritual children, St. Padre Pio answered: "*The Rosary*." He would often say, "In books we *seek* God, in prayer we *find* Him. Pray, hope, and don't worry."

The other saint mentioned was St. Louis de Montfort, who faithfully prayed the Rosary every day and urged people to do the same. This energetic Third Order Dominican believed that priests who follow the example of St. Dominic by praying the Rosary every day, preaching it unceasingly and urging others to pray it daily, would bear much fruit and do great good for souls. In his brilliant book, *The Secret of the Rosary*, he stressed that the heavenly gift of the Rosary must not be neglected, for experience has shown that both sin and disorder spread far and wide when the Rosary is neglected. According to a 2001 poll by the Center for Applied Research for the Apostolate, the majority of Catholics in the U.S. do not pray the Rosary on a regular basis. We can see so clearly, in the U.S. and worldwide, the dire consequences of this neglect. St. Louis de Montfort—*please* pray for us!

St. John Paul II looked to all of us to rediscover the Rosary in the light of Scripture. His splendid method has Biblical foundations (see Ch.6) that will help us in this rediscovery. He marvelously wrote about the Rosary being an aid to ecumenism if it is properly revitalized, and how it can help sustain the Liturgy and enable people to participate more fully and interiorly in it. He asked his brother bishops, priests, and deacons to rediscover the beauty of the Rosary. He asked them, through their own personal experience of its beauty, to promote it with conviction. At the end of his letter, he wrote, "I look to all of you, brothers and sisters of every state, to you, Christian families, to you, the sick and elderly, and to you, young people: *confidently take up the Rosary again.* May this appeal of mine not go unheard" (no. 43).

Finally, let us try to remember what Benedict XVI told the young in Australia at the 2008 World Youth Day. He said, "Side by side with material prosperity, a spiritual desert is spreading and an interior emptiness."[11] The Rosary, the school of Mary, well-presented and properly prayed, will bring down the dew of divine grace onto this spiritual desert, this barren soil, and be the very means of satisfying the thirst of so many who are interiorly empty. This will lead to the new "springtime of the human spirit" that St. John Paul II had predicted. He also strongly believed that the Rosary, a sweet "chain" which links us to God, is destined at the dawn of the third millennium to bring forth a harvest of *holiness*.

Chapter 3
Fatima and the Rosary

Mary appeared in Fatima, Portugal, in 1917 to three children. She called herself the *Lady of the Rosary*. She appeared to Jacinta, age seven, Francisco, her brother, age nine, and Lucia, their cousin, age ten. She appeared to them on six occasions from May 13 to October 13, 1917. On October 13, 1917, she stated, "I am the Lady of the Rosary. I want a chapel built here in my honor. Continue to pray the Rosary every day." Jacinta was later questioned and asked what was the chief thing Mary told Lucia. Her reply was, "That we should pray the Rosary every day." Dr. Carlos Mendes, who questioned all three children during the apparitions, stated, "The principle thing that emerges, according to my own analysis, is that the Lady wishes the spread of devotion to the Rosary."[12] In her apparitions Mary urged, with great insistence, that we pray the Rosary every day.

On May 13, 1982, St. John Paul II went to Fatima with a Rosary in hand to thank Mary for her protection during the attempt on his life one year earlier in St. Peter's Square, during which he was shot and almost bled to death. He was convinced that, as he said, "It was a 'mother's hand' that guided the bullet's path and the Pope halted at the threshold of death."[13] The shrine at Fatima possesses one of the bullets that was fired at the Pope on May 13, 1981. It has been embedded in the crown that adorns the statue of Our Lady of Fatima. While at Fatima, St. John Paul II said, "Do you want me to tell you a secret? It is simple: pray very much. Pray the Rosary every day. The Lady of the message points to the Rosary, which can rightly be defined as 'Mary's prayer,' the prayer in which she feels particularly united with us."[14] Before leaving Fatima for Rome on May 13, he went back in the late afternoon to the chapel of the apparitions. He took his Rosary and went into deep contemplation. He prayed at the exact hour that he was shot in Rome one year earlier. In his letter on the Rosary, he mentioned Fatima as an occasion in which Mary "made her presence felt and her voice heard, in order to exhort us to this form of contemplative prayer" (no. 7).

The oldest of the children, Lucia, became Sister Lucia and

Mary came to Fatima in 1917 and appeared to these three children: Jacinta, Lucia, and Francisco. In each of the six apparitions, Mary urged that we pray the Rosary every day in order to obtain world peace and an end to war.

lived for many years as a Carmelite nun in a Carmelite convent in Coimbra, Portugal. She died February 13, 2005, at the age of 97. Cardinal Tarcisco Bertone, the former Secretary of State for the Holy See, had three meetings with her. The Cardinal has stated that Sister Lucia once said, "The Rosary is the most beautiful prayer heaven has taught us. More than any other prayer it leads us to a better knowledge of God and his redemptive work."[15] She believed that after the Mass, the Rosary is what most unites us to God. Sister Lucia analyzed Mary's message and has shared it with us. In her book, *"Calls" from the Message of Fatima*, she states, "Those who give up saying the Rosary and who do not go to daily Mass, have nothing to sustain them, and so end up by losing themselves in the materialism of earthly life. We must pray the Rosary every day because we need to pray and we must do so. Our Lady insists that we pray the Rosary every day because she knows our inconstancy, our weakness and our need."[16]

On July 13, 1917, at Fatima, Mary spoke to Lucia regarding devotion to the Immaculate Heart as a means of saving souls and obtaining peace. On December 10, 1925, Mary appeared to her, now Sister Lucia, in her convent at Pontevadra, Spain, and explained to her the form that this devotion would take. Mary asked that on each First Saturday of the month we pray 5 decades of the Rosary and also keep her company for 15 minutes, meditating on the mysteries of the Rosary (Ch.6), with the intention of making reparation for the offenses against her Immaculate Heart. She also asked that we receive Holy Communion and go to Confession on each First Saturday for the same intention.

On July 13, 1917, at Fatima, Mary told the three children, "In the end, my Immaculate Heart will triumph. The Holy Father will consecrate Russia to me and she shall be converted and a period of peace will be granted to the world." In regard to her prophecy, "The Holy Father will consecrate Russia to me," this consecration was done by St. John Paul II on March 25, 1984. On November 8, 1989, Sister Lucia personally confirmed that this consecration by the Pope corresponded to what Mary wished. The fulfillment of the last part of the prophecy, "She (Russia) shall

Sister Lucia, seen here with St. John Paul II at Fatima, stated: "All well-intentioned people can, and should, recite the five decades of the Rosary every day. The Rosary should constitute each person's spiritual food."

be converted and a period of peace will be granted to the world," depends on us, that is, doing our part of praying the Rosary every day and practicing the "First Saturday Devotion" each month. It is interesting to note that Sister Lucia once wrote, "The practice of the devotion of the First Saturdays, together with the consecration to the Immaculate Heart of Mary, will determine whether there is to be peace or war in the world."[17]

On his visit to Fatima May 13, 2010, Benedict XVI expressed a wish: "May the seven years which separate us from the 100th anniversary of the apparitions (2017) hasten the fulfillment of the prophecy of the triumph of the Immaculate Heart of Mary to the glory of the Most Holy Trinity."[18] On other occasions throughout his papacy, Benedict XVI taught us that at Fatima Mary *insistently recommended* the daily praying of the Rosary. Benedict XVI exhorted us to accept Mary's request and pledge to pray the Rosary for peace in families, nations, and the world.

In Mary's apparition on May 13, 1917, Mary requested that "… the Rosary be prayed every day in order to obtain peace for the world and the end of the war." In St. John Paul II's letter on the Rosary, he wrote that he was entrusting the cause of peace to the praying of the Rosary. He wrote that his predecessors and he had many times proposed the Rosary as a prayer for peace. He also wrote, "The Rosary is by its nature a prayer for peace, since it consists in the contemplation of Christ, the *Prince of Peace*, the one who is 'our peace.' The Rosary allows us to hope that even *today*, the difficult 'battle' for peace can be *won*" (no. 40).

St. John Paul II mentioned that there is a great need today to implore from God the gift of peace. He wrote, "A number of historical circumstances make a revival of the Rosary quite timely" (no. 6). In the wake of the 2001 terrorist attack in New York City, St. John Paul II stated on September 30, 2001, "I appeal to all, individuals, families, and communities, to pray the Rosary for peace, even daily, so that the world will be preserved from the dreadful scourge of terrorism."[19] He stated in his letter that the challenges confronting the world at the start of the third millennium lead us to think that only an intervention from on high can give reason to hope for a brighter future. Like Mary at Fatima, St. John Paul II exhorted us to turn to the Rosary in seeking this *divine* intervention and so obtain the "sunshine" of God's peace.

Chapter 4
The Rosary and Contemplation

In his Apostolic Letter, *For the New Millennium*, St. John Paul II challenged the Church to launch out "into the deep" in the 3rd millennium, beginning with the contemplation of the face of Christ. The Rosary is a way of contemplating the face of Christ, seeing him—we may say—with the eyes of Mary. The late Holy Father continually stressed that the Rosary is the privileged path to contemplation. It is *"Mary's way."*

When praying the Rosary, we pray like Mary, following the method of prayer that she practiced; she kept all the memories of her Son's life in her heart and *pondered* over them. St. John Paul II wrote in his letter that those memories of Jesus, impressed upon her heart, were to be the "rosary" which Mary prayed throughout her earthly life. He also noted in his letter that when we pray the Rosary, we "enter into contact with the memories and the contemplative gaze of Mary" (no. 11).

As our mother and teacher, Mary so wants the Rosary to have a sanctifying effect on us. In his letter, St. John Paul II wrote, "Mary constantly sets before the faithful the 'mysteries' of her Son, with the desire that the contemplation of those mysteries will *release* all their saving power" (no. 11). On his 2008 trip to Lourdes, Benedict XVI stated, "When we pray the Rosary, Mary offers us her heart and her gaze in order to contemplate her Son, Jesus Christ." [20]

In his letter, St. John Paul II stated, "The Rosary, precisely because it starts with Mary's own experience, is an exquisitely contemplative prayer. Without this 'contemplative dimension,' it would lose its meaning, as Pope Paul VI clearly pointed out: 'Without contemplation, the Rosary is a body without a soul'" (no. 12). Meditation is the *soul* of the Rosary; just as the human soul gives life to the body, so meditation on the mysteries (Ch. 6) gives life to the Rosary. The restoring of this "contemplative dimension" surely has the potential of revitalizing the Rosary in the 21st century. St. John Paul II's new method, explained in Ch. 5 and detailed in its application in Ch. 6, will surely help people experience the Rosary as a contemplative prayer. This experience is open to all. In 2008, Benedict XVI stated, "The Rosary is a *contemplative* prayer accessible to all, great and small, lay people and clerics, cultured and uncultured."[21]

St. John Paul II was very concerned about the absence of meditation and the contemplative life in our culture. In 2003, he told the youth in Madrid, Spain, "The drama of contemporary culture is the lack of interiority, the absence of contemplation; without interiority, culture has no content. It is like a body that has not found its soul. Mary is the best teacher for achieving knowledge of the truth through contemplation. I invite you to be part of the 'School of Mary.' She is the model of contemplation and a wonderful example of fruitful, joyful, and enriching interiority. She will teach you never to separate action from contemplation." He encouraged us to meditate on the mysteries of Christ, in the Rosary, as seen through Mary's *eyes* and to relive them in her motherly *heart*. He continually encouraged us to pray and contemplate with Mary, in her company, like the Apostles did when they were in the Upper Room at Pentecost.

St. John Paul II prayed that Mary would join the Church, as she did at Pentecost (Acts 1:14), in praying for a new outpouring of the Holy Spirit, which in turn, would launch a "new evangelization." He often spoke of the Rosary as a prayer that we pray with Mary as the Apostles in the Upper Room prayed with her, preparing themselves to receive the Holy Spirit. This praying of the Rosary, *with* Mary, could surely bring about a "new Pentecost." Today, our homes, schools, and churches can be "upper rooms" where we pray the Rosary—the "JPII Method"—*with* Mary and prepare ourselves to receive the Holy Spirit. And then, under the Spirit's impulse, we would "set out into the deep" with a "new evangelization" that would set the 21st. century on fire.

St. John Paul II masterfully wrote in his letter that when the Rosary combines *all* the elements needed for an effective meditation (see Ch. 6), we present *Our Lady of the Rosary* with an opportunity to continue her work of proclaiming Christ and to relate to us her personal account of the Gospel. St. John Paul II's new method of praying the Rosary, described in Chapters 5 and 6 of this book, will surely help us to develop such an effective meditation. Mary will be so grateful for our making the effort for her to have an opportunity to proclaim and joyfully show her Son to us.

Chapter 5
The John Paul II Method

1. Opening Prayers

St. John Paul II mentions that it is, in some places, customary to begin the Rosary with words of Psalm 70:

"O God, come to my aid;
O Lord, make haste to help me"

He states that these words "nourish in those who are praying a humble awareness of their own insufficiency" (no. 37). After saying these words of Psalm 70, the Glory Be would then be recited. Following the Glory Be, the person would then begin to meditate on the Rosary mysteries. He also stated that, in other places, the Rosary begins with the Apostles Creed, "as if to make the profession of faith the basis of the contemplative journey about to be undertaken" (no. 37). He noted that either custom is an equally legitimate *way* to begin the Rosary.

2. Using the Rosary Beads

As a simple counting mechanism, St. John Paul II noted that "the beads mark the succession of Hail Marys and that they converge upon the crucifix. The life and prayer of believers is centered upon Christ" (no. 36). In his letter, he quoted Blessed Bartolo Longo who saw the beads "as a 'chain' which links us to God" (no. 36). The late Pope described this chain "as a 'sweet chain', for sweet indeed is the bond to God who is also our Father" (no. 36).

3. Announce Each Mystery

In announcing each mystery, the words direct the imagination and the mind toward a particular episode in the life of Christ. St. John Paul II recommends that we use a picture or an icon to "open up a scenario" on which to focus our attention. A picture helps us use our imagination to visualize ourselves as onlookers in the mystery. He mentioned that making use of visual and imaginative elements (*composition of place*) was proposed by St. Ignatius of Loyola and judged to be of great help in focusing the mind on a particular mystery. Pictures appear in Ch. 6.

4. Listening to the Word of God

St. John Paul II stated in his Rosary letter, "In order to supply a Biblical foundation and greater depth to our meditation, it is helpful to follow the announcement of the mystery with the proclamation of a related Biblical passage" (no. 30). Ch. 6 will assist us in this. St. John Paul also states, "No other words can ever match the efficacy of the inspired word. As we listen we are certain that this is the word of God, spoken for *today* and spoken 'for me.' It is not a matter of recalling information, but of allowing God to speak" (no. 30).

5. Silence

In the same letter, St. John Paul II stated, "Listening and meditation are nourished by silence. A discovery of the importance of silence is one of the secrets of practicing contemplation and meditation" (no. 31). He wrote that it is fitting to pause briefly or for a suitable amount of time after meditating on the Word of God so that the mind can *focus* on the content of the mystery. He stressed the importance of doing this before reciting the decade of prayer. Moreover, Benedict XVI called the Rosary "a school of contemplation and silence." He also taught that the Rosary, as a contemplative prayer, can't happen without an atmosphere of *inner* silence following the meditation. In silence the voice of God speaks to us like a "still small voice" of a gentle breeze as mentioned in 1 Kings 19:12. Practice this method of silence after each meditation as detailed in Ch. 6.

6. The "Our Father"

St. John Paul II noted, "after focusing on the mystery, it is natural for the mind to be lifted up toward the Father" (no. 32). He wrote that the Our Father acts as a kind of foundation for the meditation on Jesus and Mary which unfolds in the Hail Mary. He wrote that "in each of his mysteries, Jesus always leads us to the Father. He wants us to share in his intimacy with the Father, so that we can say with him: 'Abba Father'" (no. 32). *The Catechism of the Catholic Church* states "praying the Our Father develops a humble and trusting heart that enables us to turn and become like children, for it is to 'little children' that the Father is *revealed*" (CCC 2785).

7. The Ten "Hail Marys"

St. John Paul II wrote that in praying the first part of the Hail Mary we acknowledge the greatest miracle in history—the Incarnation of the Son in Mary's womb—and share in God's own wonderment as he contemplates his "masterpiece." Mary's prophecy here finds its fulfillment: "Henceforth all generations will call me blessed" (LK 1:48). He noted that "by making our *own* the words of the Angel Gabriel and St. Elizabeth contained in the Hail Mary, we find ourselves constantly drawn to seek out afresh in Mary, in her arms and in her heart, the 'blessed fruit of her womb'" (no. 24).

St. John Paul II mentioned that the center of gravity in the Hail Mary, the hinge as it were which joins its two parts, is the name of Jesus. He stressed that when we pray the Hail Mary "in a hurried recitation, this center of gravity can be overlooked, and with it the connection to the mystery of Christ being contemplated" (no. 33). He also stressed that "the emphasis given to the name of Jesus and to his mystery is the sign of a meaningful and fruitful praying of the Rosary" (no. 33). He referred to the custom of mentioning the name of Jesus in the Hail Mary, followed by the addition of a clause, referring to the mystery being contemplated. He added that using clauses is a praiseworthy custom, especially in public recitation, and an aid in our concentration, helping us enter more deeply into the mystery of Christ. Clauses are used in Ch. 6.

8. The "Gloria"

The praise of the Holy Trinity is the goal of all Christian contemplation. St. John Paul II wrote that the *Gloria*, the high point of contemplation, be given due prominence in the Rosary. He recommended that it be sung in public recitation as a way of giving proper emphasis to the Holy Trinity, our life's destiny and deepest longing. He added that this prayer "raises the mind as it were to the heights of heaven...a foretaste of the contemplation yet to come" (no. 34).

On Benedict XVI's 2008 trip to Lourdes, he mentioned that as Mary watched Bernadette pray the Rosary, she united herself with Bernadette and prayed the *Glory Be* with her, while bowing her head. He said that this confirms the "God-centered" character of the Rosary. Upon Bernadette finishing the Rosary, Mary *smiled.*

9. Prayer for Fruits or Virtues

St. John Paul II instructed us in his letter that the contemplation of the mysteries could better express their full spiritual fruitfulness if an effort were made to conclude each mystery with a prayer for the fruits specific to that particular mystery. In this way, he thought the Rosary would better express its connection with the Christian life. These fruits to be prayed for appear in Ch. 6. Mary requested at Fatima in 1917 that we pray the following prayer at the end of each decade: "O my Jesus, forgive us, save us from the fire of hell. Lead all souls to heaven, especially those who are most in need" (Apparition on July 13, 1917).

10. The Closing Prayer

St. John Paul II recommends that we end the Rosary with a prayer (customarily an Our Father, Hail Mary, and Glory Be) for the Pope's intentions, which can be expanded to include all the needs of the Church. He also taught us that praying the Hail Holy Queen or Litany of Loretto at the end is the crowning moment of a journey that has led us into living contact with the mystery of Jesus and Mary.

11. The Weekly Schedule

St. John Paul II recommended the following schedule:

> Monday: Joyful Mysteries
> Tuesday: Sorrowful Mysteries
> Wednesday: Glorious Mysteries
> Thursday: Mysteries of Light
> Friday: Sorrowful Mysteries
> Saturday: Joyful Mysteries
> Sunday: Glorious Mysteries

On October 19, 2008, at the world-famous Rosary Shrine in Pompeii, Italy, Benedict XVI stated, "Those who, like Mary and with her, cherish and ponder the mysteries of Jesus assiduously, increasingly assimilate his sentiments and are conformed to him."[24] All 20 mysteries will be covered in Ch. 6 using the *John Paul II Method*, which Benedict XVI encouraged all of us to practice.

Chapter 6

The 20 Mysteries

1st Joyful Mystery
The Annunciation

Gabriel's greeting to the Virgin of Nazareth is linked to an invitation to messianic joy: "Rejoice, Mary" (JPII's Rosary letter, no. 20).

The Word of God: Luke 1:26-38

1. In the sixth month the angel Gabriel was sent from God to… a virgin betrothed to a man whose name was Joseph … and the virgin's name was Mary.

2. And he came to her and said, "Hail, full of Grace, the Lord is with you!"

3. But she was greatly troubled at the saying, and considered in her mind what sort of greeting this might be.

4. And the angel said to her, "Do not be afraid, Mary, for you have found favor with God."

5. "And behold, you will conceive in your womb and bear a son, and you shall call his name Jesus."

6. "He will be great, and will be called the Son of the Most High;… and he will reign over the house of Jacob forever."

7. And Mary said to the angel, "How can this be, since I have no relations with a man?"

8. And the angel said to her, "The Holy Spirit will come upon you, and the power of the Most High will over shadow you."

9. "Therefore the child to be born will be called holy, the Son of God."

10. "Behold I am the handmaid of the Lord; let it be done to me according to your word."

Silent Reflection

Fruit to pray for: A share in Mary's faith; a heart open to God

Clause used in Hail Mary: Jesus, incarnate in Mary's womb

Decade: Gloria sung in public, Fatima prayer

2nd Joyful Mystery

The Visitation

With Elizabeth, the sound of Mary's voice and the presence of Christ in her womb caused John to "leap for joy" (JPII's Rosary letter, no. 20).

The Word of God: Luke 1:39-49

1. In those days Mary arose and went with haste into the hill country, to a city of Judah, and she entered the house of Zechariah and greeted Elizabeth.

2. And when Elizabeth heard the greeting of Mary, the baby leaped in her womb.

3. Elizabeth was filled with the Holy Spirit and she exclaimed with a loud cry, "Blessed are you among women, and blessed is the fruit of your womb!"

4. "And why is this granted me, that the mother of my Lord should come to me?"

5. "For behold, when the voice of your greeting came to my ears, the babe in my womb leaped for joy."

6. "And blessed is she who believed that there would be a fulfillment of what was spoken to her from the Lord."

7. And Mary said, "My soul magnifies the Lord, and my spirit rejoices in God my Savior."

8. "For he has regarded the low estate of his handmaiden."

9. "For behold, henceforth all generations will call me blessed."

10. "For he who is mighty has done great things for me, and holy is his name."

Silent Reflection

Fruit to pray for: Charity—love of God and neighbor

Clause used in Hail Mary: Jesus, who did great things for Mary

Decade: Gloria sung in public, Fatima prayer

3rd Joyful Mystery
The Birth of Jesus

Gladness fills the scene in Bethlehem, when the birth of the divine Child, the Savior of the world, is announced by the song of the angels and proclaimed to the shepherds as "news of great joy" (JP II's Rosary letter, no. 20).

The Word of God: Luke 2:4-19

1. And Joseph also went up from Galilee,... to the city of David, which is called Bethlehem ... to be enrolled with Mary his betrothed, who was with child.
2. And she gave birth to her first-born son and wrapped him in swaddling cloths and laid him in a manger, because there was no room for them in the inn.
3. And in that region there were shepherds out in the field, keeping watch over their flock at night.
4. And an angel of the Lord appeared to them, and the glory of the Lord shone around them, and they were filled with fear.
5. And the angel said to them, "Be not afraid; for behold, I bring you good news of great joy ... for to you is born this day in the city of David a Savior, who is Christ the Lord."
6. And suddenly there was with the angel a multitude of the heavenly host praising God and saying, "Glory to God in the highest, and on earth peace among men with whom he is pleased."
7. And they went with haste, and found Mary and Joseph, and the babe lying in a manger.
8. And when they saw it they made known the saying which had been told to them concerning the child.
9. And all who heard it wondered at what the shepherd told them.
10. But Mary kept all these things, pondering them in her heart.

Silent Reflection

Fruit to pray for: Humility—being a child in relation to God

Clause used in Hail Mary: Jesus, born of Mary

Decade: Gloria sung in public, Fatima prayer

4th Joyful Mystery

The Presentation of Jesus in the Temple

The Presentation not only expresses the joy of the Child's consecration; it also records the prophecy that Christ will be a "sign of contradiction and a sword will pierce his mother's heart" (JP II's Rosary letter, no. 20).

The Word of God: Luke 2:22-35
Matthew 2:1-2; 2:11

1. And when the time came for their purification ... they brought him up to Jerusalem to present him to the Lord.

2. Now there was a man ... whose name was Simeon, and this man was ... looking for the consolation of Israel.

3. And it had been revealed to him by the Holy Spirit that he should not see death before he had seen the Lord's Christ.

4. When the parents brought in the child Jesus...Simeon took him up in his arms and blessed God.

5. Simeon said, "Lord, now lettest thou thy servant depart in peace, according to thy word."

6. "For mine eyes have seen thy salvation which thou hast prepared in the presence of all peoples, a light for revelation to the Gentiles, and for glory to thy people Israel."

7. Simeon blessed them and said to Mary his mother, "Behold, this child is set for the fall and rising of many in Israel, and for a sign that is spoken against."

8. "And a sword will pierce through your own soul also."

9. Wise men from the East came to Jerusalem, saying, "Where is he who has been born king of the Jews? For we have seen his star in the East, and have come to worship him."

10. And going into the house they saw the child with Mary his mother, and they fell down and worshipped him.

Silent Reflection

Fruit to pray for: To be self-giving—to live for others

Clause used in Hail Mary: Jesus, model of self-giving

Decade: Gloria sung in public, Fatima prayer

5th Joyful Mystery

The Finding of Jesus in the Temple

Joy mixed with drama marks the fifth mystery, the finding of the twelve-year old Jesus in the Temple. Here he listens and raises questions, already in effect one who "teaches" (JP II's Rosary letter, no. 20).

The Word of God: Luke 2:41-51

1. Now his parents went to Jerusalem every year at the feast of the Passover.... And when the feast was ended, as they were returning, the boy Jesus stayed behind in Jerusalem.
2. His parents did not know it, but supposing him to be in the company they went a day's journey.
3. They sought him among their kinfolk and acquaintances; and when they did not find him, they returned to Jerusalem, seeking him.
4. After three days they found him in the temple, sitting among the teachers, listening to them and asking them questions.
5. All who heard him were amazed at his understanding and his answers. And when Mary and Joseph saw him they were astonished.
6. His mother said to him, "Son, why have you treated us so? Behold, your father and I have been looking for you anxiously."
7. And he said to them, "How is it that you sought me? Did you not know that I must be in my Father's house?"
8. And they did not understand the saying which he spoke to them.
9. And he went down with them and came to Nazareth, and was obedient to them.
10. His mother kept all these things in her heart.

Silent Reflection

Fruit to pray for: Justice—giving God and others their just due

Clause used in Hail Mary: Jesus, one who "teaches"

Decade: Gloria sung in public, Fatima prayer

1st Mystery of Light
Christ's Baptism in the Jordan

The Baptism in the Jordan is first of all a mystery of light.
Here, Christ descends into the waters, the innocent one who
became "sin" for our sake (JP II's Rosary letter, no. 21).

The Word of God: Matthew 3:1-17

1. In those days came John the Baptist, preaching in the wilderness of Judea, "Repent, for the kingdom of heaven is at hand."

2. Then went out to him Jerusalem and all Judea and all the region about the Jordan.

3. They were baptized by him in the river Jordan, confessing their sins.

4. John said, "I baptize you with water for repentance, but he who is coming after me is mightier than I;… He will baptize you with the Holy Spirit and with fire."

5. Then Jesus came from Galilee to the Jordan to John, to be baptized by him.

6. John would have prevented him, saying, "I need to be baptized by you, and do you come to me?"

7. But Jesus answered him, "Let it be so now; for thus it is fitting for us to fulfill all righteousness."

8. And when Jesus was baptized, he went up immediately from the water, and behold, the heavens were opened.

9. He saw the Spirit of God descending like a dove, and alighting on him.

10. Lo, a voice from heaven, saying, "This is my beloved Son, with whom I am well pleased."

Silent Reflection

Fruit to pray for: To *train in holiness* through meditation (Ch.6)

Clause used in Hail Mary: Jesus, beloved of the Father

Decade: Gloria sung in public, Fatima prayer

2nd Mystery of Light
The Wedding Feast of Cana

The first of signs, given at Cana, when Christ changes water into wine and opens the hearts of the disciples to faith, thanks to the intervention of Mary, the first among believers (JP II's Rosary letter, no. 21).

The Word of God: John 2:1-11

1. On the third day there was a marriage at Cana in Galilee, and the mother of Jesus was there; Jesus also was invited to the marriage, with his disciples.

2. When the wine failed, the mother of Jesus said to him, "They have no wine."

3. And Jesus said to her, "O woman, what have you to do with me? My hour has not yet come."

4. His mother said to the servants, "Do whatever he tells you."

5. Now six stone jars were standing there, for the Jewish rites of purification, each holding twenty or thirty gallons.

6. Jesus said to them, "Fill the jars with water." And they filled them up to the brim.

7. He said to them, "Now draw some out, and take it to the steward of the feast." So they took it.

8. When the steward of the feast tasted the water now become wine, and did not know where it came from… the steward of the feast called the bridegroom.

9. The steward said to him, "Every man serves the good wine first; and when men have drunk freely, then the poor wine; but you have kept the good wine until now."

10. This, the first of his signs, Jesus did at Cana in Galilee, and manifested his glory; and his disciples believed in him.

Silent Reflection

Fruit to be prayed for: Gratitude—to God and to others

Clause used in Hail Mary: Jesus, changing water into wine

Decade: Gloria sung in public, Fatima prayer

3rd Mystery of Light

The Proclamation of the Kingdom of God

Another mystery of light is the preaching by which Jesus proclaims the coming of the Kingdom of God, calls to conversion, and forgives the sins of all who draw near to him in humble trust (JP II's Rosary letter, no. 21).

The Word of God: Matthew 4:13-33
Matthew 9:2
John 8:12

1. And leaving Nazareth he went and dwelt in Capernaum by the sea.

   From that time, Jesus began to preach, saying, "Repent, for the kingdom of heaven is at hand."

2. Jesus spoke to them, saying, "I am the light of the world; he who follows me will not walk in the darkness, but will have the light of life."

3. As he walked by the sea of Galilee, he saw two brothers, Simon who is called Peter and Andrew his brother, casting a net into the sea. And he said to them, "Follow me, and I will make you fishers of men."

4. And Jesus went about all the cities and villages, teaching in the synagogues and preaching the gospel of the kingdom, and healing every disease and infirmity.

5. "You are the light of the world. Let your light so shine before men, that they may see your good works and give glory to your Father who is in heaven."

6. And behold, they brought to him a paralytic, lying on his bed; and when Jesus saw their faith he said to the paralytic, "Take heart, my son; your sins are forgiven."

Silent Reflection

Fruit to be prayed for: Conversion (seeking God) and humble trust in God's infinite mercy

Clause used in Hail Mary: Jesus, light of the world

Decade: Gloria sung in public, Fatima prayer

4th Mystery of Light

The Transfiguration

The Mystery of light par excellence is the Transfiguration,
traditionally believed to have taken place on Mount Tabor.
The glory of the Godhead shines forth from the face of Christ.
(JP II's Rosary letter, no. 21).

The Word of God: Matthew 17:1-8

1. And after six days, Jesus took with him Peter and James and John his brother, and led them up a high mountain apart.

2. And he was transfigured before them, and his face shone like the sun.

3. His garments became white as light.

4. And behold, there appeared to them Moses and Elijah, talking with him.

5. And Peter said to Jesus, "Lord, it is well that we are here; if you wish, I will make three booths here, one for you and one for Moses and one for Elijah."

6. He was still speaking, when lo, a bright cloud overshadowed them.

7. A voice from the cloud said, "This is my beloved Son, with whom I am well pleased; listen to him."

8. When the disciples heard this, they fell on their faces, and were filled with awe.

9. But Jesus came and touched them, saying, "Rise, and have no fear."

10. And when they lifted up their eyes, they saw no one but Jesus only.

Silent Reflection

Fruit to be prayed for: To be a light to the world—allow Jesus to been seen through us

Clause used in Hail Mary: Jesus, whose face shined like the sun

Decade: Gloria sung in public, Fatima prayer

5th Mystery of Light
The Institution of the Eucharist

The institution of the Eucharist, in which Christ offers his body
and blood as food under the signs of bread and wine, and
testifies "to the end" his love for humanity, for whose salvation
he will offer himself in sacrifice (JP II's Rosary letter, no. 21).

The Word of God: John 6: 51-56
Luke 22:8-20

1. "I am the living bread which came down from heaven; if any one eats of this bread, he will live forever; and the bread which I shall give for the life of the world is my flesh."

2. So Jesus said to them…"He who eats my flesh and drinks my blood has eternal life, and I will raise him up at the last day."

3. "For my flesh is food indeed, and my blood is drink indeed. He who eats my flesh and drinks my blood abides in me, and I in him."

4. So Jesus sent Peter and John, saying, "Go and prepare the Passover for us, that we may eat it."

5. And when the hour came, he sat at table, and the apostles with him.

6. And he took bread, when he had given thanks he broke it and gave it to them, saying, "This is my body which is given for you."

7. "Do this in remembrance of me."

8. And likewise the cup after supper, saying, "This cup which is poured out for you is the new covenant in my blood."

Silent Reflection

Fruit to be prayed for: A deep faith in, and devotion to, the Eucharist

Clause used in Hail Mary: Jesus, bread of life

Decade: Gloria sung in public, Fatima prayer

1st Sorrowful Mystery

The Agony in the Garden

The sequence of meditations begins with Gethsemane. There Jesus encounters all the temptations and confronts all the sins of humanity, in order to say to the Father: "Not my will but yours be done" (JP II's Rosary letter, no. 22).

The Word of God: Luke 22:39-44
Matthew 26:37-46

1. And he came out, and went as was his custom, to the Mount of Olives; and the disciples followed him.
2. And when he came to the place he said to them, "Pray that you may not enter into temptation."
3. And taking with him Peter and the two sons of Zebedee, he began to be sorrowful and troubled.
4. Then he said to them, "My soul is very sorrowful, even to death; remain here, and watch with me."
5. And he withdrew from them about a stone's throw, and knelt down and prayed.
6. "Father, if thou art willing, remove this cup from me; nevertheless not my will, but thine, be done."
7. And there appeared to him an angel from heaven, strengthening him.
8. And being in an agony he prayed more earnestly; and his sweat became like great drops of blood falling down upon the ground.
9. And he came and found them sleeping, and he said to Peter, "Simon, are you asleep? Could you not watch one hour? Watch and pray that you may not enter into temptation; the spirit indeed is willing, but the flesh is weak."
10. "Behold, the hour is at hand, and the Son of man is betrayed into the hands of sinners. Rise let us be going; see, my betrayer is at hand."

Silent Reflection

Fruit to be prayed for: Perseverance in prayer and meditation

Clause used in Hail Mary: Jesus, in his agony

Decade: Gloria sung in public, Fatima prayer

2nd Sorrowful Mystery

The Scourging at the Pillar

This "Yes" of Christ reverses the "No" of our first parents in the Garden of Eden. And the cost of this faithfulness to the Father's will is made clear by his scourging (JP II's Rosary letter, no. 20).

The Word of God: Matthew 27:11-26

1. Now Jesus stood before the governor; and the governor asked him, "Are you the king of the Jews?" Jesus said to him, "You have said so." But when he was accused by the chief priests and elders, he made no answer.

2. Then Pilate said to him, "Do you not hear how many things they testify against you?" But he gave him no answer.

3. Now at the feast the governor was accustomed to release for the crowd any one prisoner whom they wanted.

4. And they had then a notorious prisoner, called Barabbas.

5. The governor again said to them, "Which of the two do you want me to release for you?" And they said, "Barabbas."

6. Pilate said to them, "Then what shall I do with Jesus who is called Christ?" They all said, "Let him be crucified."

7. So when Pilate saw that he was gaining nothing, but rather that a riot was beginning, he took water and washed his hands before the crowd.

8. Pilate said, "I am innocent of this righteous man's blood; see to it yourselves."

9. And all the people answered, "His blood be on us and on our children!"

10. Then he released for them Barabbas, and having scourged Jesus, delivered him to be crucified.

Silent Reflection

Fruit to pray for: Respect and care for the body and chastity; Temperance—moderate the attraction of pleasures

Clause used in Hail Mary: Jesus, scourged at the pillar

Decade: Gloria sung in public, Fatima prayer

3rd Sorrowful Mystery

The Crowning of Thorns

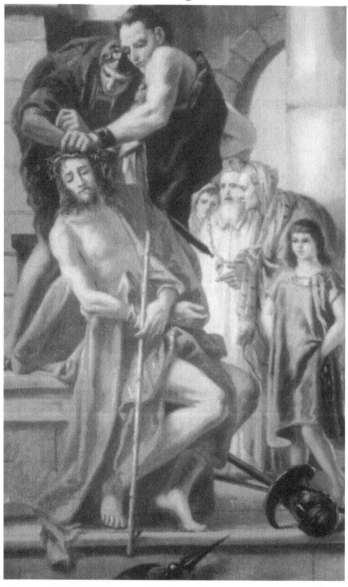

Ecce homo (Behold the man): the meaning, origin and fulfilment
of man is to be found in Christ, the God who humbles himself
out of love "even unto death, death on a cross" (JP II's Rosary
letter, no. 22).

The Word of God: Mark 15:16-20

1. And the soldiers led him away inside the palace (that is, the praetorium).

2. They called together the whole battalion.

3. And they clothed him in a purple cloak.

4. And plaiting a crown of thorns they put it on him.

5. And they began to salute him, "Hail, King of the Jews!"

6. And they struck his head with a reed.

7. And spat upon him.

8. And they knelt down to homage him.

9. And when they had mocked him they stripped him of the purple cloak, and put his own clothes on him.

10. And they led him out to crucify him.

Silent Reflection

Fruit to be prayed for: Prudence—making good decisions; using practical reason to discern our true good

Respect—for life; for the dignity of the human person; for work

Clause used in Hail Mary: Jesus, crowned with thorns

Decade: Gloria sung in public, Fatima prayer

4th Sorrowful Mystery
The Carrying of the Cross

This faithfulness to the Father's will is made clear in the carrying of the cross (JP II's Rosary letter, no. 22).

The Word of God: Luke 23:26-31
Mark 15:20-23

1. And the soldiers led him out to crucify him.
2. And as they led him away, they seized one Simon of Cyrene, who was coming in from the country.
3. They laid on him the cross, to carry it behind Jesus.
4. And there followed him a great multitude of the people, and of women who bewailed and lamented him.
5. But Jesus turning to them said, "Daughters of Jerusalem, do not weep for me, but weep for yourselves and for your children."
6. "For behold, the days are coming when they will say, 'Blessed are the barren, and the wombs that never bore, and the breasts that never gave suck!'"
7. "Then, they will begin to say to the mountains, 'Fall on us'; and to the hills, 'Cover us.'"
8. "For if they do this when the wood is green, what will happen when it is dry?"
9. And they brought him to the place called Golgotha (which means the place of a skull).
10. And they offered him wine mingled with myrrh; but he did not take it.

Silent Reflection

Fruit to be prayed for: Fortitude—become a sharer, through your suffering, in the redemptive suffering of Christ—unite your suffering to the cross

Clause used in Hail Mary: Jesus, carrying the cross

Decade: Gloria sung in public, Fatima prayer

5th **Sorrowful Mystery**

The Crucifixion

The sorrowful mysteries help the believer to relive the death of
Jesus, to stand at the foot of the Cross beside Mary, to enter with
her into the depths of God's love for man and to experience all
its life-giving power (JP II's Rosary letter, no. 22).

The Word of God: Luke 23:33-46
John 19:26-30

1. And when they came to the place which is called The Skull, there they crucified him, and the criminals, one on the right and one on the left.

2. And Jesus said, "Father, forgive them; for they know not what they do."

3. One of the criminals who were hanged railed at him, saying, "Are you not the Christ? Save yourself and us!"

4. But the other rebuked him…And he said, "Jesus, remember me when you come in your kingly power."

5. And he said to him, "Truly, I say to you, today you will be with me in Paradise."

6. When Jesus saw his mother, and the disciple whom he loved standing near, he said to his mother, "Woman, behold, your son!" Then he said to the disciple, "Behold, your mother!"

7. And about the ninth hour Jesus cried with a loud voice…"My God, my God, why hast thou forsaken me?"

8. After this Jesus, knowing that all was now finished, said (to fulfill the scripture), "I thirst."

9. So they put a sponge full of the vinegar on hyssop and held it to his mouth. When Jesus had received the vinegar, he said, "It is finished."

10. Then Jesus, crying with a loud voice, said, "Father, into thy hands I commit my spirit!" And having said this he breathed his last.

Silent Reflection

Fruit to pray for: Forgiveness—for those who hurt us in any way

Clause used in Hail Mary: Jesus, crucified

Decade: Gloria sung in public, Fatima prayer

1ˢᵗ Glorious Mystery
The Resurrection

Contemplating the Risen One, Christians rediscover the reasons
for their own faith and relive the joy of Mary, who must have
had an intense experience of the new life of her glorified Son (JP
II's Rosary letter, no. 23).

The Word of God: Matthew 28:1-9

John 20:19-23

1. Now after the sabbath, toward the dawn of the first day of the week, Mary Magdalene and the other Mary went to see the sepulchre.
2. And behold, there was a great earthquake.
3. An angel of the Lord descended from heaven and came and rolled back the stone, and sat on it.
4. So they departed quickly from the tomb with fear and great joy, and ran to tell his disciples.
5. And behold, Jesus met them and said, "Hail!" And they came up and took hold of his feet and worshiped him.
6. On the evening of that day…the doors being shut where the disciples were, for fear of the Jews, Jesus came and stood among them and said to them, "Peace be with you."
7. When he had said this, he showed them his hands and his side.
8. Jesus said to them again, "Peace be with you."
9. He breathed on them, and said to them, "Receive the Holy Spirit."
10. "If you forgive the sins of any, they are forgiven; if you retain the sins of any, they are retained."

Silent Reflection

Fruit to pray for: Hope—"hope is always linked to the future; it is the expectation of future good things" –JPII

Clause used in Hail Mary: Jesus, risen from the dead

Decade: Gloria sung in public, Fatima prayer

2nd Glorious Mystery

The Ascension

In the Ascension, Christ was raised in glory to the right hand of the Father, while Mary herself would be raised to that same glory in the Assumption (JP II's Rosary letter, no. 23).

The Word of God: Acts 1:3-10
Acts 2:11-14

1. To them Jesus presented himself alive after his passion by many proofs, appearing to them during forty days, and speaking of the kingdom of God.
2. So when they had come together, they asked him, "Lord, will you at this time restore the kingdom to Israel?"
3. He said to them, "It is not for you to know times or seasons which the Father has fixed by his own authority."
4. "But you shall receive power when the Holy Spirit has come upon you."
5. "And you shall be my witness in Jerusalem and in all Judea and Samaria and to the end of the earth."
6. And when he had said this, as they were looking on, he was lifted up, and a cloud took him out of their sight.
7. And while they were gazing into heaven as he went, behold, two men stood by them in white robes.
8. The two men said, "Men of Galilee, why do you stand looking into heaven?"
9. "This Jesus, who was taken up from you into heaven, will come in the same way as you saw him go into heaven."
10. Then they returned to Jerusalem. All these with one accord devoted themselves to prayer, together with the women and Mary, the mother of Jesus, and with his brethren.

Silent Reflection

Fruit to pray for: To hope to one day be with Jesus forever

Clause used in Hail Mary: Jesus, ascended into heaven

Decade: Gloria sung in public, Fatima prayer

3rd Glorious Mystery
The Descent of the Holy Spirit

Pentecost reveals the face of the Church as a family gathered together with Mary, enlivened by the powerful outpouring of the Spirit and ready for the mission of evangelization (JP II's Rosary letter, no. 23).

The Word of God: Acts 1:3-10
Acts 2:11-14

1. When the day of Pentecost had come, they were all together in one place.
2. And suddenly a sound came from heaven like the rush of a mighty wind, and it filled all the house where they were sitting.
3. And there appeared to them tongues as of fire, distributed and resting on each one of them.
4. And they were all filled with the Holy Spirit and began to speak in other tongues, as the Spirit gave them utterance.
5. Now there were dwelling in Jerusalem Jews, devout men from every nation under heaven. And at this sound the multitude came together, and they were bewildered, because each one heard them speaking in his own language.
6. But Peter, standing with the eleven, lifted up his voice and addressed them, "Men of Judea and all who dwell in Jerusalem…this is what was spoken by the prophet Joel."
7. "And in the last days it shall be, God declares, that I will pour out my Spirit upon all flesh, and your sons and your daughters shall prophesy."
8. "Let all the house of Israel therefore know assuredly that God has made him both Lord and Christ, this Jesus whom you crucified."
9. And Peter said to them, "Repent, and be baptized every one of you in the name of Jesus Christ for the forgiveness of your sins; and you shall receive the gift of the Holy Spirit."
10. So those who received his word were baptized, and there were added that day about three thousand souls.

Silent Reflection
Fruit to be prayed for: Gifts of the Holy Spirit
Clause used in Hail Mary: Jesus, sending down the Holy Spirit
Decade: Gloria sung in public, Fatima prayer

4ᵗʰ Glorious Mystery

The Assumption of Mary

In the Assumption, Mary herself, enjoying beforehand, by a unique privilege, the destiny reserved for all the just at the resurrection of the dead (JP II's Rosary letter, no. 23).

Benedict XVI, Songs, Revelation:

1. "Mary has left death behind her; she is totally clothed in life, she is taken up body and soul into God's glory" (8/15/07).
2. "Mary was taken up body and soul into Heaven. We have a Mother in Heaven. Heaven is open, Heaven has a heart" (8/15/05).
3. "My beloved speaks and says to me: 'Arise, my love, my dove, my fair one, and come away'" (Songs 2:10).
4. "In the glory of Heaven, because she is with God and in God, she is very close to each one of us" (8/15/05).
5. "Then God's temple in heaven was opened, and the ark of his covenant was seen within his temple" (Rev 11:19).
6. "And a great sign appeared in heaven, a woman clothed with the sun" (Rev 12:1).
7. "We all need her help and comfort to face the trials and challenges of daily life" (8/15/07).
8. "By looking at Mary's face, we can see more clearly than any other way, the beauty and mercy of God" (8/15/06).
9. "Let me see your face, let me hear your voice, for your voice is sweet, and your face is comely" (Songs 2:14).
10. "In Mary's face, we can truly perceive the divine light" (8/15/16).

Silent Reflection

Fruit to be prayed for: Entrust yourself to Mary— *Totus Tuus*: "I am all yours, Mary."

Clause used in Hail Mary: Jesus, assumed Mary into Heaven

Decade: Gloria sung in public, Fatima prayer

5th Glorious Mystery

The Coronation of Mary as Queen

Crowned in glory—Mary shines forth as Queen of the Angels and Saints (JP II's Rosary letter, no. 23).

Saint John Paul II, Sirach, Proverbs:

1. "The Council explained that she was exalted by the Lord as Queen of the Universe, that she might be the more fully conformed to her Son, the Lord of lords and conqueror of sin and death" (7/23/97).

2. "When she became Mother of the Creator, she truly became queen of all creatures" (7/23/97).

3. "Who is this that looks forth like the dawn, fair as the moon, bright as the sun?" (Songs 6:10)

4. "Her queenship expresses the power conferred on her to carry out her maternal mission" (7/23/97).

5. "My throne was in a pillar of cloud, and for eternity I shall not cease to exist" (Sir. 24:4,9).

6. "She is beside us, because her glorious state enables her to follow us in our daily earthly journey" (7/23/97).

7. "For he who finds me finds life and obtains favor from the Lord" (Prov 8:35).

8. "Having a motherly affection for us, she extends her care to the whole human race" (7/23/97).

9. "Happy are those who keep my ways, watching daily at my gates" (Prov 8:35).

10. "She knows everything that happens in our life and supports us with maternal love" (7/23/97).

Silent Reflection

Fruit to be prayed for: A devotion to her Rosary as a
                                    contemplative prayer

Clause used in Hail Mary: Jesus, crowning Mary as Queen
Decade: Gloria sung in public, Fatima prayer

Appendix

HOW TO PRAY THE ROSARY

1. Make the **Sign of the Cross** and say the **"Apostle's Creed."**
2. Say the **"Our Father."**
3. Say three **"Hail Marys."**
4. Say the **"Glory be to the Father."**
5. Announce the First Mystery; then say the **"Our Father."**
6. Say ten **"Hail Marys,"** while meditating on the Mystery.
7. Say the **"Glory be to the Father."**
8. Announce the Second Mystery; then say the **"Our Father."** Repeat 6 and 7 and continue with Third, Fourth and Fifth Mysteries in the same manner.

Our Father, Who art in heaven; hallowed be Thy name; Thy kingdom come; Thy will be done on earth as it is in heaven. *Give us this day our daily bread; and forgive us our trespasses as we forgive those who trespass against us, and lead us not into temptation; but deliver us from evil. Amen.*

Hail Mary, full of grace, the Lord is with thee; blessed art thou among women, and blessed is the fruit of thy womb, Jesus. *Holy Mary, Mother of God, pray for us sinners, now and at the hour of our death. Amen.*

Glory be to the Father, and to the Son, and to the Holy Spirit. *As it was in the beginning, is now, and ever shall be, world without end. Amen.*

Prayers at the beginning and the end of the Rosary.

The Apostles' Creed

I believe in God, the Father Almighty, Creator of heaven and earth; and in Jesus Christ, his only Son, Our Lord, who was conceived by the Holy Spirit, born of the Virgin Mary, suffered under Pontius Pilate, was crucified, died, and was buried. He descended into hell; the third day He rose again from the dead. He ascended into heaven, and is seated at the right hand of God, the Father Almighty. From thence He shall come to judge the living and the dead.

I believe in the Holy Spirit, the Holy Catholic Church, the Communion of Saints, the forgiveness of sins, the resurrection of the body, and life everlasting. *Amen.*

Hail, Holy Queen

Hail, Holy Queen, Mother of Mercy, our life, our sweetness and our hope! To you do we cry, poor banished children of Eve; to you do we send up our sighs, mourning, and weeping in this valley of tears. Turn, then, most gracious advocate, your eyes of mercy towards us, and after this our exile, show unto us the blessed fruit of your womb, Jesus. O clement, O loving, O sweet Virgin Mary!

V. Queen of the Most Holy Rosary, pray for us.

R. That we may be made worthy of the promises of Christ.

Let us Pray

O God, whose only begotten Son, by His life, death, and resurrection, has purchased for us the rewards of eternal life, grant, we beseech You, that meditating upon these mysteries of the Most Holy Rosary of the Blessed Virgin Mary, we may imitate what they contain and obtain what they promise, through the same Christ, our Lord. *Amen.*

Fatima prayer at end of each decade.

"O my Jesus forgive us, save us from the fire of hell! Lead all souls to heaven, especially those who are most in need" (apparition of Mary on July 13, 1917 at Fatima).

Fifteen promises of the Blessed Virgin
to Christians who faithfully pray the Rosary

1. To all those who shall pray my Rosary devoutly, I promise my special protection and great graces.
2. Those who shall persevere in the recitation of my Rosary will receive some special grace.
3. The Rosary will be a very powerful armor against hell; it will destroy vice, deliver from sin and dispel heresy.
4. The Rosary will make virtue and good works flourish, and will obtain for souls the most abundant divine mercies. It will withdraw the hearts of men from the love of the world and its vanities, and will lift them to the desire of eternal things. Oh, that souls would sanctify themselves by this means.
5. Those who trust themselves to me through the Rosary will not perish.
6. Whoever recites my Rosary devoutly reflecting on the mysteries, shall never be overwhelmed by misfortune. He will not experience the anger of God nor will he perish by an unprovided death, but if a sinner he will be converted; if just he will persevere in grace and merit eternal life.
7. Those truly devoted to my Rosary shall not die without the sacraments of the Church.
8. Those who are faithful to recite my Rosary shall have during their life and at their death the light of God and the plenitude of His graces and will share in the merits of the blessed.
9. I will deliver promptly from purgatory souls devoted to my Rosary.
10. True children of my Rosary will enjoy great glory in heaven.
11. What you shall ask through my Rosary you shall obtain.
12. To those who propagate my Rosary I promise aid in all their necessities.
13. I have obtained from my Son that **all the members of the Rosary Confraternity** shall have as their intercessors, in life and in death, the entire celestial court.
14. Those who recite my Rosary faithfully are my children, and brothers and sisters of Jesus my only son.
15. Devotion to my Rosary is a special sign of predestination.

Confraternity of the Rosary

The Confraternity was instituted in the 13th century by St. Dominic in response to a *command* he received from *heaven* to establish it. Pope Innocent III gave St. Dominic his full approval and encouragement to preach and establish the Confraternity. Dominic established it in nearly every town that he preached the Rosary. The Confraternity is an association that is spiritually beneficial for members of all ages. Bl. Pier Giorgio Frassati became a member when he was 17 years old. Like he did, our young people today who enroll and become members will also have countless other people praying daily for them.

Mary has promised in her well-known Rosary promises: "I have obtained from my Son that all members of the Confraternity of the Rosary shall have in life and in death all the Blessed in Heaven as their intercessors." St. John Vianney said: "If any has the happiness of being in the Confraternity of the Holy Rosary, he and she have in all corners of the globe brothers and sisters who pray for them." The Dominican Order promises that all members of the Confraternity will share in their Masses, Rosaries, apostolic works, prayers, and penances. The only obligation (which does not bind under sin) for the members is to pray at least 15 decades – 3 five decade Rosaries – during the course of each week, while meditating on its mysteries, which would include and cover all the 15 traditional mysteries of the Rosary. All members pray for one another and for their intentions. If you wish to be a member of the Confraternity of the Rosary, please send your full name and address to:

Rosary Center, Dominican Fathers
P.O. Box 3617
Portland, Oregon 97208

Excerpts from John Paul II's Apostolic Letter: The Rosary of the Virgin Mary

1. The Rosary of the Virgin Mary, which gradually took form in the second millennium under the guidance of the Spirit of God, is a prayer loved by countless Saints and encouraged by the Magisterium. Simple yet profound, it still remains, at the dawn of this third millennium, a prayer of great significance, destined to bring forth a harvest of holiness.

2. With the Rosary, the Christian people *sit at the school of Mary* and are led to contemplate the beauty on the face of Christ and to experience the depths of His love. Through the Rosary the faithful receive abundant grace, as though from the very hands of the Mother of the Redeemer.

3. From my youthful years this prayer has held an important place in my spiritual life. The Rosary has accompanied me in moments of joy and in moments of difficulty. To it I have entrusted any number of concerns; in it I have always found comfort.

4. Against the background of the words *Ave Maria* the principal events of the life of Jesus Christ pass before the eyes of the soul. They take shape in the complete series of the joyful, sorrowful, and glorious mysteries, and they put us in living communion with Jesus through—we might say—the heart of his Mother.

5. To recite the Rosary is nothing other than to *contemplate with Mary the face of Christ*.

6. The Rosary, reclaimed in its full meaning, goes to the very heart of Christian life; it offers a familiar yet spiritual and educational opportunity for personal contemplation, the formation of the People of God, and the new evangelization.

7. Yet the Rosary clearly belongs to the kind of veneration of the Mother of God described by the Council: a devotion directed to the Christological center of the Christian faith, in such a way that "when the Mother is honored, the Son ... is duly known, loved and glorified." If properly revitalized, the Rosary is an aid and certainly not a hindrance to ecumenism!

8. But the most important reason for strongly encouraging the practice of the Rosary is that it represents a most effective means of fostering among the faithful that *commitment to the contemplation of the Christian mystery*, which I have proposed in the Apostolic Letter *Novo Millennio Ineunte* as a genuine "training in holiness": "What is needed is a Christian life distinguished above all in the *"art of prayer"*.

9. A number of historical circumstances also make a revival of the Rosary quite timely. First of all, the need to implore from God *the gift of peace*. The Rosary has many times been proposed by my predecessors and myself as a prayer for peace.

10. The revival of the Rosary in Christian families, within the context of a broader pastoral ministry to the family, will be an effective aid to countering the devastating effects of this crisis typical of our age.

11. Many signs indicate that still today the Blessed Virgin desires to exercise through this same prayer that maternal concern to which the dying Redeemer entrusted, in the person of the beloved disciple, all the sons and daughters of the Church: "Woman, behold your son!" (Jn 19:26).

12. I would therefore ask those who devote themselves to the pastoral care of families to recommend heartily the recitation of the Rosary. *The family that prays together stays together*. The Holy Rosary, by age-old tradition, has shown itself particularly effective as a prayer that brings the family together.

13. The Rosary mystically transports us to Mary's side as she is busy watching over the human growth of Christ in the home of Nazareth. This enables her to train us and to mold us with the same care, until Christ is "fully formed" in us (cf. Gal 4:19).

14. The Rosary is both meditation and supplication. Insistent prayer to the Mother of God is based on confidence that her maternal intercession can obtain all things from the heart of her Son.

15. When the recitation of the Rosary combines all the elements needed for an effective meditation, especially in its communal celebration in parishes and shrines, it can present *a significant catechetical opportunity* that pastors should use to advantage. In this way too, Our Lady of the Rosary continues her work of proclaiming Christ.

16. Dear brother and sisters! A prayer so easy and yet so rich truly deserves to be rediscovered by the Christian community.

17. What is really important is that the Rosary should always be seen and experienced as a path of contemplation.

18. When prayed well in a truly meditative way, the Rosary leads to an encounter with Christ in his mysteries and so cannot fail to draw attention to the face of Christ in others, especially in the most afflicted.

19. At the same time, it becomes natural to bring to this encounter with the sacred humanity of the Redeemer all the problems, anxieties, labors, and endeavors which go to make up our lives. "Cast your burden on the Lord and he will sustain you" (Ps 55:23). To pray the Rosary is to hand over our burdens to the merciful hearts of Christ and his Mother.

20. It is only in the mystery of the Word made flesh that the mystery of man is seen in its true light. The Rosary helps to open up the way to this light.

21. In the spiritual journey of the Rosary, based on the constant contemplations—in Mary's company—of the face of Christ, this demanding ideal of being conformed to him is pursued through an association which could be described in terms of friendship.

22. The Rosary is also a path of proclamation and increasing knowledge, in which the mystery of Christ is presented again and again at different levels of the Christian experience. Its form is that of a prayerful and contemplative presentation, capable of forming Christians according to the heart of Christ.

23. The Rosary is one of the traditional paths of Christian prayer directed to the contemplation of Christ's face. Pope Paul VI described it in these words: "As a Gospel prayer, centered on the mystery of the redemptive Incarnation, the Rosary is a prayer with a clearly Christological orientation."

24. The contemplation of Christ has an incomparable model in Mary. In a unique way, the face of the Son belongs to Mary.

It was in her womb that Christ was formed receiving from her a human resemblance which points to an even greater spiritual closeness.

25. No one has ever devoted himself to the contemplation of the face of Christ as faithfully as Mary.

26. The eyes of her heart already turned to him at the Annunciation, when she conceived him by the power of the Holy Spirit. In the months that followed, she began to sense his presence and to picture his features. When she gave birth to him in Bethlehem, her eyes were able to gaze tenderly on the face of her Son, as she "wrapped him in swaddling cloths, and laid him in a manger" (Lk 2:7).

27. Thereafter Mary's gaze, ever filled with adoration and wonder, would never leave him. At times it would be a questioning look, as in the episode of the finding in the Temple: "Son why have you treated us so?" (Lk 2:48); it would always be a penetrating gaze, one capable of deeply understanding Jesus, even to the point of perceiving his hidden feelings and anticipating his decisions as at Cana (cf. Jn 2:5).

28. At other times, it would be a look of sorrow, especially beneath the cross, where her vision would still be that of a mother giving birth, for Mary not only shared the passion and death of her Son, she also received the new Son given to her in the beloved disciple (cf. Jn 19:26-27).

29. On the morning of Easter, hers would be a gaze radiant with the joy of the resurrection, and finally, on the day of Pentecost, a gaze afire with the outpouring of the Spirit (cf. Acts 1:14).

30. The Rosary, though clearly Marian in character, is at heart a Christocentric prayer. In the sobriety of its elements, it has all the depth of the Gospel message in its entirety, of which it can be said to be a compendium.

Notes

1. Gabriel Hardy, O.P., *Rediscovering the Rosary*, Veritas Publications, Dublin, Ireland, 1983, p. 9.
2. Valentine Long, O.F.M., *The Mother of God*, Franciscan Herald Press, Chicago, IL, 1976, p. 128.
3. Cardinal Tarcisio Bertone, *The Last Secret of Fatima*, Doubleday, NY, NY, 2008, p. 2.
4. *L'Osservatore Romano,* Vatican City, May 7, 2008, p. 2.
5. Robert Feeney, *The Catholic Ideal:Exercise and Sports*, Aquinas Press, Alexandria, VA, 2005, p.167.
6. *L'Osservatore Romano*, Vatican City, April 20, 2011, p.13.
7. *L'Osservatore Romano*, March 19, 2003, p. 7.
8. Ibid., p. 7.
9. Robert Feeney, *The Rosary: The Little Summa*, Aquinas Press, Alexandria, VA, 2003, p. 67.
10. L'Osservatore Romano, May 5, 1999, p. 1.
11. L'Osservatore Romano, July 23, 2008, p. 13.
12. John De Marchi, I.M.C., *Fatima: The Full Story*, 1986, p. 245.
13. *L'Osservatore Romano*, May 17,1982, p.3.
14. *L'Osservatore Romano*, May 17, 2000, p.3.
15. *The Last Secret*, p. 33.
16. Sister Lucia,*"Calls" from the Message of Fatima*, Secretariado dos Pastorinhos, Fatima, Portugal, 1997, p.132.
17. *The Seers of Fatima,* April/June, 1996, p. 2.
18. Benedict XVI, *Light of the World*, Ignatius Press, San Francisco, CA, 2010, p. 166.
19. *L'Osservatore Romano*, October 3, 2001, p. 2.
20. *L'Osservatore Romano*, September 17, 2008, p. 14.
21. *L'Osservatore Romano*, October 22, 2008, p.7.
22. *L'Osservatore Romano*, January 7, 2009, p. 7.
23. *L'Osservatore Romano*, October 22, 2008, p. 4.
24. Ibid., p. 4.